To everyone who has ever felt "weird"
for liking something different from others: It's okay, I'm weird too!
Embrace it. Be the weird you want to see in the world!

IMPRINT
A part of Macmillan Publishing Group, LLC
120 Broadway, New York, NY 10271

ABOUT THIS BOOK
All art for this book was digitally created in Illustrator and Photoshop using a Wacom Cintiq.
The text was set in Apercu, and the display type is Smash.
The book was edited by John Morgan and designed by Carolyn Bull.
The production was supervised by Jie Yang, and the production editor was Kathy Wielgosz.

Printed in China by RR Donnelley Asia Printing Solutions Ltd.,
Dongguan City, Guangdong Province

Library of Congress Cataloging-in-Publication Data is available.
ISBN 978-1-250-31133-7 (hardcover)

Our books may be purchased in bulk for promotional, educational, or business use.
Please contact your local bookseller or the Macmillan Corporate
and Premium Sales Department at (800) 221-7945 ext. 5442 or by email
at MacmillanSpecialMarkets@macmillan.com.

Book design by Carolyn Bull

Imprint logo designed by Amanda Spielman

First edition, 2021

1 3 5 7 9 10 8 6 4 2

mackids.com

Better not steal this book or you're in for a treat:
Panda Cat will stop by and fart all over your cheek.

IT'S OKAY TO SMELL GOOD!

JASON THARP

[Imprint]
MAKE YOUR MARK
NEW YORK

In the town of **Smellsville**,
Panda Cat's day always began the same way.
He brushed his teeth with **garlic and onion** toothpaste.
He combed **rotten eggs** into his hair.
Finally, he smeared **moldy mayonnaise** into his armpits.

Panda Cat gobbled down his breakfast of **spoiled milk**, moldy toast with **toe jam**, and a **rotten apple**.

He fed his pet stinkbug, Clarence,
placed a dozen rotten eggs out to freshen the air,
and left for school.

Panda Cat was born to be stinky, and he loved it!
He lived near *Gross and Smelly Works* and everyone
in Smellsville loved their super-stinky soaps.

At Smellsville Smellementary School,
Panda Cat greeted his friends: Binny Binturong,
Doug Dung Beetle, and Stanley Stinkbird.

"Hey, Panda Cat, you'll never believe this, but Einstink
is the guest judge at the science fair!" Binny said.

Panda Cat's personal hero, Smellbert Einstink, had discovered the ***theory of stinkativity***. And Panda Cat hoped that he could win the fair with his own smell-errific breakthrough: the stinkiest soap ever made.

After school, Panda Cat skipped stinkball practice to work on his experiment with his friends. They tried three times to make their own super-smelly breakthrough, but it just wasn't powerful enough.

"Ugh, why isn't this working?" Panda Cat asked.
"The fair's tomorrow."

"I don't know, but I gotta go," Binny said.
"My parents are taking me to see Dr. Stinkelton tomorrow
in New Fart City. They're worried I don't stink enough.
I'm really sorry I can't help more."

Doug and Stanley stayed and helped Panda Cat gather all the stinkiest things he could find: *Limburger cheese*, *rotten socks*, and a can of *grandpa farts*. Panda Cat was excited to push the limits of stink.

Suddenly, Panda Cat's beaker of liquid
turned the weirdest shade of green.
Then stink fumes began to fill the air.

Green smoke poured out
and smelled like a fresh stew of barf and dog poo!

Panda Cat smiled.
It was working!

But something changed:
The stinky green ooze began to turn pink.

And then . . . *BOOM!*

Panda Cat was covered in a pink ooze that wasn't stinky at all.
In fact, it smelled like **cotton candy** and **sugar cookies**.

"HOW DID THIS HAPPEN?" Panda Cat shouted.
"What's that smell?!" Doug shouted.
"It makes me want to barf!" Stanley said.

They ran out the door together.

This doesn't smell stinky at all, Panda Cat thought.
Now I'll never win the science fair.

But as he sat there, he didn't feel bad.
Actually, he felt kind of good.

He realized he'd never smelled anything as good as this pink stuff.

But then Panda Cat remembered
how Doug and Stanley ran away.
I don't want to lose my friends, he thought.

Panda Cat cleaned his lab and dumped all the pink stuff into the toilet.

But he gave it one last sniff.

Then he flushed.

After he wiped himself off and rolled around
in a garbage pile, Panda Cat went to bed.
"Hopefully my experiment turns out
differently tomorrow," he said to Clarence.
"I sure don't want to let Smellbert Einstink down."

After a moment, he asked, "Clarence, would you still like me even if I liked smell-good stuff?"

Clarence smiled from his spot on Panda Cat's nose.

And Panda Cat dozed off to sleep.

The next day, all the smellementary school students were very excited to see Smellbert Einstink at the fair.

But Panda Cat was still worrying about his experiment. He decided to add a new ingredient: *rafflesia*, the stinkiest flower ever.

"And what do we have here?" someone asked.

Panda Cat looked up to see Smellbert Einstink at his table. "Oh my gosh, hi!" Panda Cat said as he quickly started up his experiment for his hero.

Stinky green smoke filled the air . . .

Then **BOOM**! Pink ooze exploded all over!
Even worse, this pink ooze smelled *better* than before.
It smelled like **caramel apples** dipped in
sugar cookies, rolled in **cotton candy**,
and covered in **strawberries**!

"What is that smell?" Panda Cat heard someone ask.

"It smells good, which is gross!" someone else said.

"YUCK!" a third student shouted.

Binny arrived just as Sal Amander won
the science fair with his ear-wax recycling kit.

"I'm sorry I missed your experiment," Binny told Panda Cat. "Guess what? Turns out I just smell like **buttered popcorn** and that's normal for Binturongs. Cool, huh?"

He looked around. "Hey, what's this pink stuff? It smells so awesome! Nice job, buddy!"

"I agree," said Smellbert Einstink.

"But this was the biggest failure ever!" Panda Cat said.

"*Was* it a failure?" Einstink asked. "Binny likes it!"

"Is it weird that I do, too . . . a little?" Panda Cat asked.

"Before I discovered the theory of stinkativity, smell-good stuff was everywhere!" Einstink said. "It's actually one of my biggest regrets. I never meant for smell-good stuff to be replaced by only stinky stuff."

"Without smell-good stuff, how would we ever appreciate really stinky stuff?" Einstink asked.

"So it's okay if I like smell-good stuff?" Panda Cat asked.

"You're allowed to like whatever you like," Einstink said. "And whatever it is, I guarantee you won't be the only one."

"Hey, where can I get more of this pink stuff?" Binny asked.

Now Panda Cat starts his days in a new way.
He brushes his teeth with **peppermint toothpaste**,
but still combs rotten eggs into his hair.

He eats **cinnamon toast with butter**
(but still loves **spoiled milk**),
and he sets out a dozen **daisies** before
saying goodbye to Clarence.

His favorite thing is working with Smellbert Einstink.

Together, they're about to **break the stink barrier**.